New Elysium: The Beginnings

Sam D. White

Chapter 1

Humans love telling stories. Some are true. Some are false. Some tell of the creation of the universe. Some tell of how it will end. I have a story, one that has never been told. A story of how the universe itself almost came to an end. When evil continuously conquered good, until evil turned on itself.

In the beginning, I was just as naive as you are now. I didn't understand just how big the universe is. I never would have guessed how dark, tortured and dangerous it would become. Before I can tell you my story, I must tell you the story of a world called Zeoneradon and the Zeons who lived there.

On Zeoneradon, the people were ruled by 10 devoted Zeons, who spent their whole lives understanding and communicating with the Goddess Teraus. Teraus would appear to the 10 Zeons, who called themselves The Elders, and tell them how to live a long and peaceful life. She would only appear in her Temple, which The Elders had made their home. They wanted to be sure that they would not miss any visit from Teraus. Zeoneradon was a beautiful, botanical planet that prospered in the peace given by The Elders. However, peace and tranquility came easy to the Zeon people, for they were highly intelligent and technologically advanced people.

Teraus, over time, grew more distant and her visits became fewer. The Elders, concerned about the infrequency of their goddess' visits, began to keep a record of everything about their seemingly disappearing Goddess. Documenting all of her visits from as far back as any of them could remember and how her behavior was when she did rarely appear. After a century of dwindling visits, Teraus would appear for the final time.

"I must speak quickly, but you must understand and remember

what I say." Teraus said to The Elders. "Zeoneradon is in trouble. It may not be now but a day will come when the planet will face its doom. You must travel the universe to a planet called Earth.

There, a Zeon of innocence and grace must find a Human pure of heart and mind. But be warned! For when a Human and a Zeon fall for one another and feel love's embrace, they become bonded.

If the bond were ever to be broken, it would be fatal to the Zeon. Humans must not know you are not of their kind. Only when the two true Human and Zeon saviors find each other, there will be no more fear of bonding." The Elders stood, dumbfounded, not sure of how to respond.

Then, as quickly as she arrived she was gone. After Teraus left, The Elders talked amongst themselves. The main question going through all their minds were, why they would have to travel to a distant planet to save their planet. Although nine of The Elders were hesitant, one of them seemed eager to travel to Earth.

"I, along with my wife, will go on this journey. I will make an announcement to the Zeon people and ask for volunteers."

The next morning Elder Kret called his people to the Temple's courtyard.

"The Goddess Teraus has appeared to us and extended a mission. I, along with my wife Captain Niral, will be taking her star ship to a neighboring world called Earth. This trip will take about a month. When we arrive, we must live among them in secret and observe the Humans who inhabit it. This mission, however, is not without dangers, should a Zeon fall for a Human, they will become bonded. After they become bonded, if the bond should break, the Zeon will die." After hearing the speech, Elder Kret dismissed the Zeon people and allowed them to talk amongst themselves.

After 3 days, seventy-five Zeon volunteers boarded Captain Niral's ship to go start a new life in a strange new world.

For a month, anxious Zeon's traveled through space in search of this new world. While most were going to serve their Goddess, some came along for the thrill of adventure and the unknown.

When they arrived at the new world, Zeons were tasked to observe only, until they could spot the differences between Human and Zeons. Humans couldn't teleport anywhere, whereas Zeons could teleport around a planet's surface. Humans had to work for materials, when Zeons were able to create things with their minds. Zeons never got sick or ill, after they have lived to the end of their life they started to fade into an eternal flame. The differences were subtle and seemed easy for Zeons to live among Humans without being discovered. Zeons seemed to be the same as Humans, the only main differences that they could tell were that Zeons were more healthier and intelligent than Humans.

    Once Elder Kret was satisfied with their research, they decided to teleport down to the planet's surface. He and his wife, Captain Niral, teleported to a little city outside Pittsburgh Pennsylvania in a country called the United States of America, with their two month old daughter. The other Zeons scattered around Earth, finding a new place to call home.

Chapter 2

"Nyomi, get up! The meeting starts soon!" I opened my eyes to see the time. Ten-thirty. The meeting of the Zeons on Earth was set for noon. I sighed and yelled back, "I'm up!"

Sitting up, I tried to wake myself. I rubbed my eyes and sat on the edge of my bed for a moment. I looked over to my bedroom door and I sighed again. I leaned back and laid down in frustration, I just saw my robe I had to wear for this meeting. Being that I am a daughter of an Elder I had to dress as one. The rob was black, ugly and unflattering. I much rather wear anything else, but being that I will one day be an Elder myself, I was forced to wear it.

I knew I had to get up, so I rolled myself out of bed to get dressed. I walked over to the clock on the wall of my bedroom and stared at it. I took a slow, deep breath and closed my eyes; as I exhaled I heard the second hand slowed to a stop.

Freezing time, I was the only one of my species that could do it. It was a special ability I seem to possess. I wasn't sure why I was different in that way, but I wasn't going to complain about being able to do it.

I turned back to the robe I had to wear and just stared at it. In some ways I liked being a Zeon. However, most of the time, I'd rather be

Human. I hated the pressure of being an Elder in training. I wanted to just be a normal, blissfully ignorant Human. Oblivious to the vast universe that surrounded them. I would rather contemplate my mortal existence, wondering if there was life beyond Earth, than have the responsibility of leading a society of "Extraterrestrial" beings on Earth.

    I reached out and grabbed the robe, feeling the silk of the fabric flow through my fingertips. I slipped it over my head, allowing it to slide down my body. I sighed, looking at the hooded figure that stood staring back at me in the mirror.

    Closing my eyes, I took another deep breath and heard the tick of the clock resume. Eleven o'clock, I had an hour of alone time before everyone was due to arrive. I turned to my desk, an hour of time to waste on my computer. Sitting down in my chair, I turned to my one enjoyment that I had. The one thing I actually loved about my life, video games. These games were my safe haven, it took me to a place where the stress of the universe faded. Meeting people on these games was amazing. It didn't matter who you are, where you came from, everyone had a common goal. It made it easy to befriend so many Humans. I learned Human culture through playing these video games.

"Nyomi, are you ready?" I heard my mother yelled from down the stairs. Eleven fifty, the time has flown by.

"Yes, I'm coming!" I yelled back. Standing up, I straightened my robe and
walked out of my room. As I reached the top of the stairs I saw my mother standing at the bottom.

"Come on, they will be here soon." she said as she walked towards the den. I slowly descended the stairs, dreading the meeting and what was to come after. Zeons meet at our house every five years, and after they leave my father would go back to Zeoneradon to report to the remaining nine Elders. This year since I am now one hundred years old, my father decided I was to join him. I was nervous about this. Earth was my home planet, I had no desire to see Zeoneradon. As I made my way into the den I saw my father lighting candles around the shrine of the All Powerful Goddess Lyra who was written about in the scrolls. I didn't know much about the origins of Lyra, just that she was a descendant of Teraus.

Towards the front of the den, my mother was drawing the blinds so that no Human could see into the room.

One by one the Zeons of Earth appeared into the den. After everyone arrived, my father stood in front of them all and my mother and I stood in the back.

"Everyone here?" my father asked as he scanned the room. "Ok, lets begin with reports of Human contacts you have had." One by one Zeons stood up and talked about the encounters they have had with humans since the last meeting. Hours passed as I stood day dreaming. I'd rather be anywhere else.

"Nyomi?" I looked up and saw my father and the other Zeons looking at me. "Your report?" he asked.

"Oh, yeah." I responded as I walked to the front to join my father. "I have befriended a Human couple. They have taught me alot about humanity. The female Human is an artist and the male is a professor. They are both smart and compassionate people." I went on to explain what art was, considering the Zeon people were too intelligent to be creative. Most seemed intrigued by the idea, whereas others saw it as a waste of time.

 After the meeting ended, I went back to my room and threw my robe on the floor. I had to pack for the month long journey ahead of me tomorrow. Instead of packing though, I decided to go see my best friend. I changed into Human clothes and went down the stairs. I figured I would walk instead of teleporting, because I felt like the fresh air would be good for me. I was so frustrated with my parents, they wanted me to be this perfect Zeon Elder but I was raised on Earth. They just couldn't understand that I was stuck between two cultures. I was raised in a Zeon household, but I grew up on Earth.

As I reached my friends house though, I felt a sense of contentment because she always knew how to help me unwind. Walking up her front steps, I saw her water her plants on her front porch.

"Hey Meg." I said to get her attention.

"What's wrong with you?" She asked looking over to me. She always knew when something was going on. It was as if she could read my face and know that there was something bothering me.

"It's nothing really, my father's making me go on a two month business trip. I leave tomorrow." I explained. To Megan, my father was a businessman and one day I will take over his company. It was the easiest way to explain without telling her who I
really was.

Megan was a beautiful Human, and the most kind and compassionate person I had ever met. Our personalities matched perfectly, which made me feel like life on Earth was the life I was meant to have.

"Doesn't that sound fun." she said sarcastically. "So what new, other then your father screwing with your life?" She asked.

"Nothing honestly. I spend too much time shadowing my father to take his place." I sighed.

"Nyomi, I know you're caught up in what your father wants you to do, but what do you want to do? You need to live your own life." Meg's words hit me hard. I just have been accepting my life when I could be controlling it.

"You're right." I said rolling my eyes.

"Of course I am." she said laughing. I smiled and hugged her. Her friendship meant alot to me. I lived one hundred years here and I had not one friend until I met this wonderful outspoken, generous friend.

"Where's John?" I asked looking around.

"Oh he is in class right now." She responded.

"So girls night on the computer?" I asked with a smirk. Megan and John also played video games which meant I spent all of my time with them, even if it wasn't in person.

"Sounds like a plan to me!" She said laughing.

Chapter 3

The next morning, I was woken up to my father pounding on my door.

"I'm up, I'm up!" I yelled as I buried my face in my pillow. It was time to go to Zeoneradon, and I'd rather just lay here. I slowly got out of bed and grabbed the bag I had packed for the trip. I looked in the mirror and rolled my eyes.

"Let's get this over with." I said under my breath.

When I teleported to the ship, I went straight to my quarters. I had no desire to socialize with any of the Zeons on the ship. Most of the Zeons that had come to Earth were born and raised on Zeoneradon, there were very few Zeons around my age. This being said, most of the Zeons would not understand my lifestyle. There was very little I knew about our culture and I was ok with that. Others, however, would look down on an Elder's decedent who knew so little about the culture. In my mind, locking myself away in my quarters was the only way not to shame my father. The ship was not very big but I know it was something my mother was proud of. She would not join us on this journey back home. My mother, being married to an Elder, would be the next person in charge of the Zeons on Earth.

    Days blurred together as I spent most of my time staring out my window. Taken notice of every star and planet we passed. Space was so peaceful, flying between the stars felt magical. When you grow up on Earth, you spend most summer nights staring up at the night sky and now I am part of the sky now.

    About a week into our journey, I was in the mess hall eating some food when I saw the most amazing sight of my life. I looked up from my food and dropped my fork in amazement. Standing up, I walked over to the window. The colors were breathtaking.

"It's beautiful isn't it?" I heard a voice say behind me.

"What is it?" I asked as I continued to stare. I felt someone walk up next to me. I could see the hooded shadow in my peripherals.

"Just a nebula, one of the last ones." The hooded figure responded.

"One of the last ones?" I asked.

"There used to be hundreds, but as worlds die, as does everything else." They said sighing.

"Worlds die?" I asked as I looked over. I then took a step back when I saw that no one was there. I started to look around to see if I could see any hooded people around me. I was alone, other than the cooks in the kitchen. My stomach became queasy as I tried to make sense of what just happened. I turned back to the nebula and sighed.

When I got back to my quarters, I saw my father sitting at his computer.

"Something strange just happened." I said to him.

"Oh?" He said not turning from the computer. I walked over to the couch and sat down. I took a deep breath before I continued.

"I was in the mess hall… and… well… I was looking at the nebula we had passed…"

"There was no nebula," My father said interrupting me looking up from the computer. He seemed concerned. He slowly stood up and walked over to me. "Then what happened?" He asked crossing his arms.

"Well... there was a nebula and, well... there was someone talking to me... but then there wasn't." I looked down at my hands, realizing how crazy I was sounding.

"I think you're just tired and your mind is playing tricks on you. I think you should get some sleep." He said standing me up and walking me to my room. I was confused. He seemed concerned about what I told him, and I knew what I saw. I was not making it up! However, I also didn't want to make myself sound even more crazy. I just sat on my bed, looking out the window at the stars that filled the space around us.

Chapter 4

"Nyomi this is Zeoneradon!" My father excitedly said. I looked at the view screen with amazement. I wanted to hate this planet but looking at it made it hard. As the ship descended below the cloud line, orange and red trees covered the planet's surface. They resembled the Earth tree in the fall. I didn't know much about Zeoneradon, but I did know that the climate stayed warm year round due to the binary suns.

Roofs of houses and buildings peeked out of the top of the tree line. It looked as if the towns were built in the amber forest. Then, I see a huge building standing alone with a large courtyard surrounding it. In the front of the building stood a giant shrine to Lyra.

After the ship had landed, I walked straight toward the shrine. It was beautiful. Blue petaled flowers on vines hung from the domed roof over the shrine. They also wrapped around the pillars that held the roof up. Getting closer to Lyra, I saw an inscription on the base.

The All-Powerful Goddess Lyra

The one true savior of the universe And great granddaughter of the Goddess Teraus

I had never seen a shrine like this and it was amazing. I found myself getting swept up in the aroma of the fresh Zeoneradon air. I then felt my father walk up behind me.

"Are you ready?" He asked. I sighed and nodded. We walked up the courtyard to the stairs of the huge building. Reaching the door my father placed the palm of his hand where normally there would be a knob. He held it there for a few seconds and the door opened.

"They have this here so that only Elder could enter at will. This is the one place Teraus would appear." He explained as he walked in. Inside the building there was a vast dimly lit hall with blue flames on either side. "These are the flames of the Elders come to pass." he continued to explain. The flames themselves floated above a black, small mount of some kind. As we got further down the hall the mounts were empty. They were the ones that had yet to be filled. Someday my eternal flame will be left here, which to me, was unsettling.

 Finally when we reached the door at the end of the hall my father stopped and turned to me.

 "This is just a learning experience for you, do not speak

unless spoken to." He said, I simply nodded. I had no desire to speak anyway.

Walking into the room there was a single spot light that shone in the middle of the room. Above, sat nine Zeons in throne-like chairs. It was as if they were looking down on us. They sat quietly, waiting for us to walk into the spotlight.

"What is your report?" The Head Elder asked.

"Well," my father started. "No Zeon has bonded yet." Before my father could finish speaking, the Head Elder cut him off.

"So you continue to fail." I looked over to my father who kept calm.

"We have gathered a lot.." and before he could finish he was interrupted again.

"Information is not what we need, and you know that." The Head Elder seemed to be agitated. "Maybe we should send another team to Earth and recall yours." After he said that I became angry.

"That's not fair, Earth is my home. It's been the home of eighty four Zeons for one hundred years." I yelled up to the Elders. I looked over to my father, hoping he would agree with me. Instead a look of disappointment swept across his face.

"Young lady! You obviously have never been told of the true nature of this mission. The universe itself has begun to spiral, we have noticed three planets already destroyed." After The Elder had said I stood in silence. "You have five year before you are recalled. Times up Kret." After The Head Elder said that, they all got up and left. I turned to my father.

"What is our mission then?!" I yelled angrily at him. My father just turned and walked back towards the door. I was so angry because I felt lied to and I knew my father was angry too. Unfortunately, my father was actually mad at me more than the Elders discussion, which angered me more. As I followed my father out the door and it closed behind us, my father turned to me.

"That was very disappointing." He started to say.

"They have no right to make us leave Earth!" I added trying to shift the anger from me to The Elders.

"No!" He yelled. "I told you not to speak unless spoken to!" I stopped and stared at him. I couldn't understand why he wasn't angry about having to abandon a mission he has been on for a hundred years. I was also upset about not knowing the true nature of the mission that is forced on me from the moment I could talk.

"What's the mission?" I asked him.

"As an Elder we agreed it would be best not to tell Zeons the true nature of our mission, in fear of it causing a mass panic." He tried to explain.

"But I'm an Elders decedent. I have the right to know!" I could see my father becoming more angry with me. He turned away from me and walked down the hall towards the front door. I started to wonder where he was going, if we were headed back home or if he was taking me to a more private place to yell at me.

My father and I have never seen eye to eye. We have always butted heads about my future and I wasn't letting up. I had always wished he understood that I would never be this perfect Elder he wanted me to be. My mother was the only one I felt close to. She was the only one who seemed to understand my passion for Humanity.

Leaving Teraus's Temple, my father walked down the path, past the ship. He stayed silent as we walked by a row of houses. The houses here on Zeoneradon did not look like the ones back on Earth. They looked metallic and were larger than most I've seen. The more houses I saw, I started to realize that there were no door knobs used here. Zeons all used their hand prints to open the doors.

Also, there were only footpaths, no roads of any kind. I guess because

Zeon's could teleport, there would be no need for vehicles. Looking at the trees that from above looked orange and red now glowed blue, like the eternal flames we saw in the Temple. They were everywhere but not so much that the sun could not shine through. Beams of golden light found its way through the leaves and flooded the beautiful world below it. The warmth of the binary suns made this world feel like a hot summer's day every day.

    While I was admiring the trees, I saw small, fluffy squirrel-like animals jumping from branch to branch. The golden color of them made them visible against the blue hue of the leaves. The chirping of them was peaceful and magical. As I was watching one of them hop through the branches, it stopped. It seemed to have spotted me. I continued to follow my father as this creature and I seem to be in a stare off. His eyes were wide and deep blue, they seemed to be just as curious about me as I was about them. Zeoneradon was a beautiful and magical planet, I couldn't deny that I like it here.

    As I was admiring my surroundings, passing multiple houses, I saw my father turn to walk up to one of the houses. Placing his hand on the door like he did with the Temple, the door opened and I followed him inside. Once inside my father turned to me with rage in his eyes and I knew this would not end well.

"You are a disappointment. Never will you EVER talk to an Elder the way you have!" He yelled in a way I have never seen before. I had never seen my father this angry, but I was just as angry to think I would be losing my home.

"I am an ELder! I deserve the same respect. I should know what is going on. I am old enough to understand whatever is going on, I am not a child anymore." I yelled back standing my ground.

"You are an Elder." My father said agreeingly. He calms himself down and continued talking. "An

Elder never questioned what their mission is. An Elder is respectful and I have never known you to be respectful at all about Zeon culture." He stopped and just let out a sigh. I was speechless. "You are to never be an Elder. You are a disappointment as a daughter." As those words left his lips I felt a hurt I have felt far too often. He turned and I stood watching him walk away into another room of the house. I sighed, and scanned the room out of curiosity. I had no idea where we were. On the wall next to the front door there was a photo hanging. In the photo was my parents with a young Zeon male. I walked into the sitting room and saw another photo of my parents and the male Zeon. I realized this was their home here on Zeoneradon. I picked up the photo and put it in my pocket. I turned back to the door and saw my father walking out of the room he was in. He stayed silent and walked straight out the front door.

    After we got back to the ship, I went into the mess hall to get some food. I also just wanted to do something to get my mind off of things. I didn't want to be an Elder in the first place and now I didn't have to. I could do my own thing, live on Earth. Then why did I feel so guilty? I felt like I had let my father down, I let the Zeon people down. Being a child of two cultures, I was unwilling to give up both of them. I felt like they were fighting over my life, but one side just gave up on me.

"Hello." I heard someone say to me. I looked up from my food to see a young male Zeon standing next to my table holding his food.

"Hi." I responded as I continued eating.

"I'm Rhygel, I heard you grew up on Earth." He smiled at me as he sat in the chair across from me.

"I'm guessing you did too?" I asked.

"Yeah, I sure did." He laughed. "But every five years I travel with Elder Kret and my parents to Zeoneradon to see our home planet and spend time with our family." I laughed under my breath. I knew since he was a Zeon who believes his home planet was Zeoneradon and not Earth, he wouldn't understand how I feel.

"This is my first year." I said.

"Oh, so you are Nyomi then!" He said excitedly, which made me feel uneasy.

"Ya, but I am just Nyomi. I am not the Elder everyone thinks I am." I said as not to get into it with him.

"Sounds like you have had a rough day. You can talk about it if you want to, or not, you don't have to. I mean if you don't want to." His way of talking made me laugh. He was all over the place and hyper.

"It's a long story." I said as to brush it off.

"Well how long is it? I mean we do have a month. I have the time, if you do."

Chapter 5

After I got back home, my mother tried talking to me about the trip but I just locked myself away in my room. I turned to my video games, the one thing I truly love. Every time I played, I always enjoyed the company of one Human. Reaper was someone who was brutally honest and outspoken, like Megan but in a goofier way. He always said what was on his mind. I decided to jump on to see if he was playing. When I went to invite him into a party, I noticed he was in a party with someone else.

"Well look who it is, decided to come back did ya?" Reaper said laughing.

"Ya I just got home today." I responded. I did tell him I was leaving for two months, he just loved to give me a hard time. "You up for some Zombies?" I asked. Reaper and I loved to play this game that you had to survive in a post apocalyptic world as long as you could, while fighting off zombies. It was a game Reaper and I played all the time.

"You play Zombies?" I heard a voice ask. It was a Human accent I had never heard before. It caught me off guard and captured my attention all at the same time. It had a draw to it that made me want to hear more.

"Yeah, and who are you?" I asked.

"My name's Colin." He responded to me.

"I just met this guy today." Reaper added.

"Oh, ok, where are you from?" I asked

"I'm from Ireland." Colin said while laughing as if he was amused by me asking. I wasn't sure what it was about this Human, but I was drawn to him. His humor mixed with an accent that mesmerized me. We spent most of the day playing together and it was the most fun I've had in a long time. He made me laugh, which was an amazing feeling after the rough couple months I had endured. I didn't want to stop talking to him.

"That's it for me guys, I have to get to bed." Colin said.

"Yeah, I'm going to get off to." I said as I logged off. I went to stand up and I saw Colin sent me a message. I sat back down and opened up the message.

It was very nice to meet you today, let's play again soon.

I smiled and replied,

Any time.

I turned to my bed and went to lay down. Colin was just a Human, but I was drawn to him. I couldn't explain it, he made me smile and laugh. I couldn't get him out of my mind.

The next morning, I sprung up out of my bed and went straight to my computer. Colin was already on so I joined him. Most of my days went like this, I woke up and played some games with Colin. I wanted to try and get to know him better. Alot of days it was just Colin and I on, although Reaper, Megan and John would jump on with us when he had the time.

After a week had passed, Megan showed up at my house.

"Hey stranger." she said as she walked into my room. I turned around and took my headset off.

"Hey." I said back to her.

"So where have you been?" She asked since we really haven't had a heart to heart since I got home.

"Well the trip was fun." I said sarcastically.

"So what happened." She stood waiting for me to answer. I tried to think of a way to explain it to her.

"Well on the trip, I got upset and raised my voice to my father." I finally said.

"Well," she paused. I could tell she was thinking of the right thing to say. "What else is going on?"

"I met a guy." When I said that her face lit up. I had never been known to show any interest in any guy and she had always pushed me to find one. "He's sweet and funny." I started to say.

"Is he cute?" She asked. I paused, not knowing what to say. I hadn't seen his face yet, only talked to him online.

"Well, I don't know," I finally said.

"What does that mean?" I could see the confusion on her face.

"I met him on my computer." I said as I pointed to my computer behind me. I waited for a response from her, but she seemed to not know what to say. "He's from

Ireland. We have talked every day since I have been home." I added, hoping she would have a response.

"Colin? You like Colin?" She finally said, I just shrugged my shoulders. "Well just be careful." She said as she walked up and hugged me. "I have to go to work, just wanted to stop in to see if you were okay." I started to laugh as I hugged her back.

After she left, I got back on the game and realized there was a new person in the party with Colin.

"I'm back, sorry Meg came in to say hi." I said putting my head set back on.

"Welcome back." I heard the new person say.

"This is Mark." Colin said. "He is someone who also plays Zombies. I met him in the game yesterday before you got on."

"Hi, I'm Nyomi. Where in the world are you from?" I asked Mark.

"I'm from Iowa." He responded.

"Ah, I'm in Pittsburgh." I started to say. "So what game are you playing?"

"It's a survival game," Mark then went on to explain how the game works and honestly, it sounded like fun. We ended up playing the rest of the day. The game was an open world game, so soon enough I was meeting more new people. I was learning so much more about humanity by playing this new game.

It was a game where you could just do nothing but still enjoy playing it. Wild creatures called Dinosaurs roamed free and we could tame them. Dinosaurs, I came to learn, were creatures that existed before Humans. Building a base was my favorite though, being as creative as I could. I wasted so much time in this game.

 Although my focus was still on Colin. I wanted to get to know him, maybe meet him. I decided to message him privately to ask if we could video chat at some point. To my surprise, he agreed. We both logged off the game and I sat nervously in front of my computer screen. What if he wasn't what I expected or I was not what he expected. My stomach started to feel funny and my face flushed.

Finally I saw the call pop up, and I froze. I took a deep breath to try and collect my nerves. I reached out to my mouse and clicked to accept it. There he was, smiling at me. His blue eyes drew me in, I was mesmerized. His smile was infectious which made me smile right away.

"Well hello," I said to him smiling.

"Hi," he responded. He seemed nervous as well. I was caught off guard by how attractive he was. I didn't want to stop talking to him. He made me laugh, made all the pain of my family life melt away. Although

I knew how dangerous it was for a Zeon and a Human to fall for eachother, I was quickly falling for him. He told me about life in Ireland, which was strange to me living in the U.S. that Ireland was so different. In Zeoneradon, the whole planet was ruled by The Elders. The whole planet was run the same way, where on Earth it was not. On Earth the different regions had wars over the Gods they follow. Zeoneradon followed Teraus's law and we all lived harmoniously.

    We talked so long that neither of us realized the time, and since Ireland was five hours ahead of where I lived, it was morning for him by the time we both went to bed.

Chapter 6

As the weeks went on, I had spent all my time either on my video games or with Megan. I was quickly making friends. I started to see Mark and others I was meeting as part of my life now as well; especially because my relationship with my mother and father seem to have dwindles to just living in the same house together. It was quiet around the house. My mother seemed to be stuck in the middle between her love for my father and her "love" for me. She wanted me to embrace the Zeon culture, which I had no interest in, and my father didn't want me to be apart of it any more. In his eyes, I was a disgrace to the life he lived and unworthy of the Elder titles. There were days where I couldn't stand to be in the house, which were the days I spent with Megan at her house.

"So how are you and Colin?" Megan asked me as she sat down next to me.

"Well we talk every day, and we video chat most nights." I responded. I was so happy with the relationship I had with Colin. He was unlike anyone I had ever met, Human or Zeon.

"So you have seen what he looks like?" She asked.

"Yes!" I said excitedly. "He has these blue eyes that just melts me every time I see them. His smile is so infectious and he makes me laugh. I love talking to him." Megan just stared at me with this small but obvious smirk. "What?!" I asked not knowing why she found that so amusing.

"You love him, don't you." She said teasingly. I didn't want to say that I was falling for a Human, because it was dangerous to do so, but I may have been doing just that.

"I don't know." I said awkwardly. "I've never been in love before."

"You love him." She said laughing.

"I haven't actually met him yet, so I really can't say. I do like him though." I wasn't just trying to convince her that I didn't love him, I was trying to convince myself. For as old as I was, I had never shown any interest in guys of any race but for some reason Colin was different. Megan, though seemed to either believe me or just decided to change the subject.

"So how are things at home?" She asked.

"Well my father hasn't talked to me since he told me I was a disgrace. My mother spends most of her days in her study. I am either here at your house or on my computer with you guys." I explained.

"And Colin." she added.

"Yes and him." I laid myself back on the couch and let out a loud sigh. "I just don't know what to do. I feel like I am meant for so much more than just my father's predecessor. Although, I let down my family because I can't be who he wants, I just couldn't see myself happy following in his footsteps. When I talk with my mother, she seems not to want to discuss it at all." I looked over to Megan, who had gone from laughing to complete silence. "I just don't know." I added to fill the silence. Megan just let out a big sigh. She stood up and grabbed a photo that was on her end table. She looked at it for a second and handed it to me.

"This is my mother and I. We haven't talked in seven years. She was toxic to my life and I am a happier person without her. Family isn't always the one you are born into. Sometimes family are people you choose to love and the love is returned without hesitation. Don't waste your time wondering what you could have done more to receive love, but spend your time wondering how you got so lucky to have someone love and care for you beyond what you think you deserve." I looked up at her and was speechless. Her advice is what I treasured the most about our friendship. She had a way of wording things in a way that touched your heart and your mind. I started to tear up.

"You are my family." I said as I felt a tear fall from my eyes.

"I am glad you feel that way." She said and she sat down on the couch and pulled me in for a hug. I placed my head on her shoulder as I wrapped my arms around her back.

"Thank you so much for being my friend." I said as I pulled away. "And with that I should be heading home." I added as I wiped the tears from my face.

"Text me when you get home." I chuckled after she said that. She always made me do that to make sure I was safe at home.

After I got home, my father met me at the front door.

"You need to see something." He said to me as he turned and walked away. As I followed him up the stairs, I texted Megan to tell her I was home. I was looking at my phone, following my father's feet, I didn't realize we had walked into their bedroom. When I looked up and saw my mother lying on the bed, looking frail. She had a low, blue light around her. I dropped my phone, as I froze, staring at her. Zeons do not get sick, they live their life in till the end. Then they fade into a blue eternal flame. My mother was dying.

I slowly walked over to her side as her head followed, watching me come closer. I fell to my knees as I reached the side of her bed. I was so stupid. I spent the past two weeks being so upset with my father and Zeon culture, I didn't see I was losing time with my mother.

"We have to travel back to Zeoneradon." My father said.

"I'm coming with you." I said as I wiped the tears away.

"No, you will stay here." He said to me. I jumped up and turned to him.

"This is my mother, our differences aside, I will be there for the release of her eternal flame." I said as calmly as I could. He stood staring at me for a moment before he nodded to agree that I should be there. Whether he was disappointed or not, my father wouldn't want to be embarrassed about my 'failures'. My father then went to call a meeting of the Zeons of Earth, to tell them they would be flying back to Zeoneradon.

When he left the room, I knelt back down next to my mother.

"Mother," I said softly, holding back my tears. She struggled to lift her arm and grab my hand. She was cold to the touch, as I could feel the life being drained from her body.

"This is only the beginning, my sweet girl. This is only the start of a story as old as time itself." She struggled to say. I held her hand tight. How is her death a start to anything? "I will always be proud of the woman you have and will become." She added as she smiled at me. My vision started to blur from the tears that filled my eyes. What could she have been proud of? I spent all my time resisting my father and hiding away in my room. My heart began to hurt to think that I would be losing the only person I could truly trust. As much as I loved my friends, none of them knew the true me, the Zeon me.

    I held my mother's hand so tight as I used my other hand to wipe the tears from my face.

"I love you Mother, I am so sorry." My voice trembled as I spoke through the pain and tears.

"You have no reason to be sorry, just continue to be you."

Chapter 7

"As a life passes, a flame lives on. As Niral starts her journey to Elysium, to live among the Goddess Teraus and the All-Powerful Goddess Lyra, a new light shines amongst us all. Niral, as you travel to Elysium, send the love of loved ones come to pass. Your flame will live on among us as a reminder of the new life you have provided for all the Earth dwelling Zeons."

I looked out amongst the thousands of Zeons gathered to witness the passing of my Mother. I then looked over to my father, standing tall as he continued the passing prayer. My mother's physical body fading in his arms as the blue flame burned through.

    The Head Elder walked over to my father as he finished his prayer and the flame was all that was left in my father's arms. He carried the flame towards the temple door. My father and I followed behind, turning away from thousands of Zeons that were now knelt down.

    The month that it took for us to come back to Zeoneradon, I had asked Rhygel to explain the traditions of a Zeon's death. Most Zeon's that die, their families have a private ceremony and their blue flame goes off, out into the world. Their flame would join the nature around them, which is what gave the trees such a beautiful blue glow.

My mother, even though she was not an Elder, was a starship captain who took the Zeons of Zeoneradon to a new home on Earth to complete a Goddess's mission. To the Elders, she earned the right to rest in the Temple. The other native Zeons that came, came to witness the first ever non-Elder to be placed in Teraus's Temple. They are were knelt in respect as she took her place amongst the Elders

When we reached an empty stand, the Head Elder knelt down to place the flame above it. When she was placed, I inscribed:

Captain Niral
Mourned by Husband Elder Kret
Survived by Nyomi

The inscription, just like the ceremony, was a Zeon tradition for when an Elder passes. Even if I wasn't happy being an Elder's predecessor, I understood and knew that this was an honor that my mother would have appreciated. As I stood up next to my father, he placed his hand on my shoulder. I think he was trying to say I had done well, without having to actually say it. We then turned and walked back out the front door.

After the ceremony for an Elder, there would be a banquet in honor of them. I went to find Rhygel, since he was the only Zeon I knew. As I searched around for him, I noticed my father talking to a Zeon who looked familiar. I stared at them, trying to maybe read their lips. They then hugged, but it wasn't a simple hug. It was a hug that was filled with pain. My father held the Zeon so tight. He had never held me in that way. So who was this Zeon, he was so familiar to me. After a couple seconds, I realized where I saw him. That Zeon was the one in all the photos I saw in my parents house. As I watched them, they turned to walk into the temple.

    When I went to follow them, Rhygel found me.

"I'm so sorry Nyomi." He said as he hugged me. I pulled away and looked over to the temple door, which was now closed. I wouldn't be able to open the door without another Elder, so I would have to wait for them to come out. "Oh, I'm sorry if that was too much?" He asked. I looked over to him and took a deep breath.

"No, sorry. I was watching my father with some other Zeon. I was just wondering who he was." I said to him.

"Oh, don't be sorry. I'm sorry I bothered you." He said while he turned to walk away.

"Rhygel." I said to stop him. "You are fine, I was actually looking for you when I spotted them." I finished saying.

"So how are you doing?" He asked.

"Ya can we go back to the ship to talk, not really comfortable around all these people." I said.

When we got back to the ship, we went into the mess hall to sit. Because everyone was still at the banquet, we were alone. I sat down and sighed.

"Here we are again, me whining to you." I said.

"I call it helping a friend." I smiled when he said that. I was remembering Megan's words before I left Earth.

"Helping family, you have become family." I said smiling.

"Well little sister, tell me what happened." He said laughing.

"Well, with the fight that my father and I had, I missed out on time with my mother. My mother was the only real family I felt I had. My father spent all his time training me to be an Elder, but my mother loved me. She spent time with me. My father and I had a fight, and I lost my mother." I looked down at my hands feeling too ashamed to look at Rhygel.

"So you feel guilty?" He asked.

"Kinda." I said, still looking at my hands.

"Why would you feel that?" I chuckled and looked up at him. "You shouldn't feel guilty. Your mother locked herself away in her study, right? She just as much shut herself away, as you did. You both needed to figure things out, you just ran out of time. You shouldn't feel guilty." He continued to say.

"Thanks. You always know how to make me laugh and feel better." I said grabbing his hand. "You're a good friend." I said smiling.

"Family, remember?"

After a while, my father and the other Earth Zeons returned to the ship. I wasted no time to seek my father out.

"Who was the guy you were talking to at the banquet?" I asked him.

"Family." He said as if not to talk about it further.

"What kind of family?" I asked.

"It's not really any of your concern. When we get home, we will have to go through your mother's things." He quickly changed the subject. I threw my hands up in the air and said,

"Why do I try with you? You can't be a father, you are just an Elder. I really wish it was you not her." I turned and walked straight to my room. I was honestly surprised he didn't follow.

When I got to my room, I bursted into tears. I completely fell apart on the floor. Crying for the loss of my mother and feared for my life to come. I didn't know what would happen when we got home. Telling my father I wish he was dead made my stomach turn. As angry as I was with him, telling him I wish he was dead hurt me. I didn't know what else to do but cry.

Chapter 8

When we got back to Earth, my phone had so many messages. Everything happened so fast, I had been gone for two month without telling anyone. As I am trying to apologize and explain how I lost my mother, I walked over to my mother's study. My father thought it would be good for me to pack it up, although I couldn't understand why it would be.

As I opened the door, which I had never been in her study before, I saw a huge bookcase next to a computer desk. I walked over to it to see the books that were on it. Reading the titles, I realized they were not books of Earth. Some were one written on Zeon, others were unknown to me. I pulled a book called, *The Age of Lyra.*

As I dusted off the cover it had appeared that the book was from Elysium. I wasn't sure what to make of it considering, Elysium was the Gods planet. So how did the book come into my mother's possession? I opened the book and combed through the pages. As I read through it, I became confused. The book described the Goddess Teruas's family. According to what I read, Teruas had a sister who was the creator and overseer of Earth. Eve apparently decided to have a child of her own, with a Human named Adam. As I read on though, I started to feel uneasy. The child would be named Abaddon, who would become known as the Demon Goddess Abaddon. Abaddon sought out to take control of all planets, even if it meant the death of all the Gods and Goddesses on Elysium.

    Reading on, Teraus also procreated with the people she created. The daughter would become known as Niral. When I read the name, goosebumped spread across my body. Niral would have a daughter named Nyomi, who was destined to bare a child of mixed heritage. I dropped the book after I read it. Taking a step back from the bookcase, I sat on the floor staring at the book. I started to tear up out of anger and sadness. Could it be a coincidence? Could I actually be a Goddess? The biggest question I had was, was my mother still alive. I got up off the floor and walked over to the computer. Turning it on, the computer seemed to scan me. When it was complete, it opened to the home screen. A message appeared on the top of the screen.

Welcome Goddess Nyomi

I was unable to move. I wasn't sure what was going on, and honestly I was scared. My hands were shaking as I reached out for the mouse. Moving the cursor to a folder marked, video dairy. Opening the folder, there were many dates going back to their first day on Earth.

"Earth date September 4th, 1915. Kret, Nyomi and I have just settled into our new home. Leaving family behind is not easy, but if the mission is successful, the universe will finally be safe. The age of Lyra is not too far off." After the video ended the next one started. "Earth date September 20th, 1915. I will be starting to do videos every year. Like a status update, you could say. Settling in was easy, we had a meeting yesterday with the Zeons who came to Earth with us. Most Zeons are uncomfortable being on a new planet, and hiding their abilities. Time will tell how our mission will progress."

I sat confused as the videos kept playing. She was so sure everything would work out. The age of Lyra is not too far off, that's what she would say. Suddenly my phone vibrated, it was Colin.

I am so sorry to hear about your mother. I have been worried about you. If you need to talk, I'm here for you.

I placed my phone back down. I needed to stay focused on whatever was going on here. I stood up from the chair and walked away from the computer. The videos kept playing behind me as I scanned the room.

As I turned back to the computer, I saw something under the desk. I moved the chair out of the way and knelt down to see what it was. It looked as if it was a small safe, but it had no handle to open it. I sat in front of the safe thinking what could be inside it. Then I thought, maybe it opened like the doors on Zeoneradon. I placed my hand on the safe and it opened instantaneously. I took a deep breath and pulled the door all the way open to see what was inside.

The safe looked empty at first but then a bright flash of light emanated from it. When the light dissipated, there was a small tablet-like object laying on the bottom. I reached in to pull it out to inspect it. The moment I held it, it turned on. The bright light flashed again to a point where all I could see was the white light.

    When the light finally faded, I was not in my mother's study anymore. I found myself standing in front of a giant waterfall. The crystal-clear water cascaded down the ledge into a pond. The surface of the water that lay still glistened from the sun shining down on it. There was a gentle breeze that blew through my hair as I stood in awe of the pure beauty that lay before me. I looked down at my hand that was still holding the tablet.

Where was I, I thought to myself. As I stood pondering, I heard a noise behind me.

"Nyomi?" I turned around to see who had called my name, and when I saw who it was I fell to my knees and cried.

"Is it really you?" I asked through the tears.

"It is." she said as she walked towards me. I stood up and fell into her arms. I held her so tight as the tears continued to fall from my eyes.

"How is this possible? I saw you fade away." I said as I pulled back to look my mother in her eyes. She smiled and wiped my tears away.

"I guess it is time for you to know who I am, who you really are."

Chapter 9

"What is going on mom?" As we sat in the grass of this beautiful place, I couldn't help but think I was dreaming. I watched her fade away. So how is it that I am sitting her with her, was she really a Goddess? Was I?

"I am not who you think I am, and in the same aspect neither are you." She responded.

"Who am I then?" I asked impatiently

"Well before I can explain that, I need to tell you where we are. I need to tell you how the universe itself was created." She paused for a moment to collect her thoughts. I started to feel a bit nervous. "Back before the universe had any life, there was one planet that did. The planet was called Elysium."

"I know about Elysium, the planet of the Gods." I interrupted.

"Yes you know of the planet, but there is so much you don't know." she continued. "Elysium itself had a ruler, her name was Torian. Torian was the first Goddess, she was the mother of all Gods and Goddess. Torian created a planet named Trydoran." She paused for a second before finishing her story. It was as if she was hesitant to finish it. She let out a deep and painful sigh before she continued. "Trydoran was the first planet to come into existence. Torian had two children born on that planet, Eve and Teruas. Teraus, as you know, created and ruled over Zeoneradon. Eve, however, created Earth. Eve fell madly in love with a Human and bore a child named Abaddon. Eve's obsession with Humans caused Abaddon to be born of obsession, which caused her to develop a sickness. She was obsessed with becoming the most powerful Goddess to ever rule. Abaddon began with creating a planet called Kreighton."

"What does any of this have to do with us?" I asked.

"You will see if you stay patient. Anyways, Kreighton was a paradise planet with a dark twist. She created an army of vicious warriors. These warriors had to be something no one would ever expect so they could protect her two sons. To this day no one has dared to step foot on the planet so no one had ever seen who or what protected them. What we did know, though, was her sons Kogg and Torg never left the planet." After she finished she seemed very nervous.

"So where does that leave us?" I asked. Nothing she had said so far had anything to do with her or me. I sat waiting impatiently wondering what this all had to do with me.

Before my mother continued, she reached out and held my hand tight.

"Teruas of Zeoneradon died a year ago to the hands of Abaddon. Which meant her oldest daughter would reign over Zeoneradon." She paused again as she teared up. I started to feel a queasy feeling in my stomach, knowing where this was going. "Teruas was my mother, your grandmother." I just stared at her not knowing how to respond.

"And this place," I started to say before my mother answered,

"Elysium. Yes we are on Elysium. You have Goddess blood in you. I know you have noticed you had abilities that Zeons do not." I was speechless. I looked around us, just trying to let everything sink in. "Unfortunately that's not the end of this story." She continued to say. "Abaddon has been trying to take over all the planets and become the sole Goddess."

"How do we stop her?" I asked. At this moment, even though everything was changing in my life, I knew that all of this was bigger than me.

"By completing the mission. You need to find the Human that will help you bring in a new age, the age of Lyra. Lyra is meant to be your daughter, with abilities we could only dream of." I stared blankly at my mother. How could so much pressure be put on me, and on a future child that I would have. My mother reached her hand out and placed it on mine.

"I know this is a lot to process but it's the only way, Nyomi." She said trying to make me feel better about what was going on.

Before I had a chance to respond a huge explosion went off in the distance and we both jumped up.

"Mom?" I said nervously. She turned to me,

"You need to go, remember what I said Nyomi. And promise me you will wait till the time is right to face Abbadon." She grabbed me by my shoulders and I could see the fear in her eyes. I nodded to her, not being able to find the words.

Another explosion went off and knocked me off my feet. I could hear screaming in the distance and my mother standing, staring at the direction of the explosions.

"You need to go!" She screamed as she held her hand up towards me. Slowly everything started to fade to black and the sound of explosions and screams became distant.

Chapter 10

Opening my eyes, I jumped up and frantically looked around. My heart was racing and I was disoriented. I was laying on the floor of my mother's study. I saw my phone laying on the floor, so I quickly picked it up. Looking at the time and date, only minutes had passed.

Sitting back on the floor, I started to cry. Was it a weird dream? It felt so real. I still had the tablet, so it had to be real. My mother was in danger, so I quickly picked up the tablet and tried going back to her.

As hard as I tried to turn the tablet on, I could not. I was even unsure of what was going on, but, at least I was learning about who I was. Not only was I a Goddess, but now I knew I had an important destiny. If I were to learn more, I would have to talk to a Zeon.

I decided to get in contact with Rhygel, he knew a lot about Zeon culture. He seemed excited to spend time with a Zeon, so he agreed without hesitation. I told him I would meet him where he lived. So after teleporting to a small town in Missouri, we met up at a local park to talk.

"How much do you know about the legend of Lyra?" I asked him sitting down at a picnic table. Rhygel sat down across from me.

"Well every young Zeon was told a story of a Demon Goddess Abaddon, who was born of obsession. This obsession grew into darkness and took her over. Her skin became cracked and the evil turned her eyes red." He started to say.

"Have you seen her?" I asked.

"No!" he said quickly. "If you met her, you will die. She shows no mercy. She decided the Gods and Goddess of Elysium were unable to keep the balance of the universe. She began killing them off, which in turn gave her the control of the planets they had watched over."

"So where does Lyra come in?" I asked.

"It is told that a child of Zeon and God bloodline would meet a human pure of heart. The child they would create would become the most powerful Goddess known, The All-Powerful Goddess Lyra. Lyra would have the power to defeat her and bring light back to a darkening universe. She will bring together the remaining Gods and Goddess and rebuild Elysium." I wasn't sure how to feel to find out that my purpose in life was to bring a child into this world, destined to lead a great battle. I felt as if it was a sacrifice more than a destiny. "Is there something wrong?" Rhygel asked.

"It seems crazy, that from the moment you're born you already have your life planned out for you." I said looking at my hand, as not to give away that I was destined to be the mother of the greatest Goddess to live.

"Everyone has a destiny, and most don't know it. Sometimes it is spelled out for you and you can just follow the path. However, some will never know the great power and bravery that they possess until it's needed the most. Who knows, maybe my destiny is to sit here at this picnic table and give you the knowledge and bravery to make a difference in this universe." Rhygel reached out and held my hand. I looked down and smiled. Somehow, those words comforted me. When I looked back up at him, he continued, "In our darkest moments of life, we can allow the darkness to consume us; or we can be the light that overcomes the darkness."

"I fear the darkness is spreading." I said pulling my hand away.

"Maybe you're the light." He responded. He stood up and walked over to the lake behind us. I turned and saw him just staring at the water. I stood up slowly and walked over to him. As I stood next to him, he did not turn. "Light is within all of us, and when it's time," He paused for a moment and looked over to me, "Your light will shine."

"How do you know?" I asked as I continued to stare at the water. Rhygel looked away.

"Faith." He said simply shrugging his shoulders. Faith was an imaginary word to me. I didn't know what was real and what was supposed to come to pass.

"Faith?" I asked as I chuckled. Rhygel grabbed me by the shoulder and turned me to him.

"Faith that you, Nyomi, will change this universe in ways none of us could ever imagine. Whether you are the foretold mother of Lyra,"
"Mother of Lyra?" I interrupted in shock.

"Or," He continued to say. "You are simply someone who will play a part in the future that I hope every day we will be able to witness ourselves." I took a deep breath and let out a subtle sigh.

"Thank you Rhygel, you have truly become a great friend." I said as I hugged him. Hearing the birds chirp around me, I turned back to the water. I watched the sun glistened off of the water's surface. I closed my eyes and breathed in the fresh air around me.

"How is it that Earth is ruled by Abaddon, yet it's so light and peaceful?" I asked taking in the warmth from the sun.

"Maybe there's someone here protecting it." Rhygel responded. I turned to him with a smirk on my face.

"How did you get so wise?" I chuckled.

"I can be wise when I want to be." He laughed back.

When I got back home, I was still unsure of what I needed to do. Rhygel's words mixed with my mother's turned and twisted inside my mind. I sat on the floor of my bedroom and cried. I cried for my mother, for the enormous burden placed on me and my future family. I cried because there was nothing else left to do, or was there?

Chapter 11

"Hello Nyomi." I looked around at a dark room. A figure stood before me, staring at me. The same hooded figure I had seen in the mess hall. The eyes, red like fire, felt as if it pierced my very soul. The cold air around us chilled me.

"Who are you?" I asked.

"I know who you are." The figure said as it stepped closer to me. As they did I took a step back to keep the distance between us. "You are destined to bring my doom, I will not allow it." I realized who they were,

Abaddon. I quickly looked around in panic.

"Where am I?" I asked as my voice quivered. Suddenly she was face to face with me, her skin was cracked and scared.

"Just remember, I am watching you."

Suddenly I sat up and realized I had fallen asleep on the floor of my room. I looked around to make sure Abaddon was not with me; I was alone. I placed my hands over my face and sat for a second. Was it all a dream? Or was it real? I felt as if my life was turning into one big delusion. I had no idea what was real anymore. If it was truly my destiny to help defeat Abaddon, I needed to do my part. The only Human that I had connected with was Colin, so I had to allow myself to feel the love I was so carefully trying to hide. I picked up my phone to text Colin.

Hey Colin, I am sorry I have been absent for so long. I have been dealing with the death of my mother and family drama.

It didn't take long for a response,

I am sorry to hear that you have been having such a rough time. I have been worried about you. Is there anything I could do for you?

It made me smile that he was concerned for me. Maybe he really was the human we spent all these years searching for. It was clear that I was the Zeon the prophecy spoke about.

There is possibly a way you can help me, I am just unsure of how to explain it.

I texted back to him. I started to get really nervous. If I was wrong about him, I could lose my life. So just like the rest of my life, I had to just have "faith" that I was doing the right thing. When I looked down at my phone, I started to shake.

No matter what it is, I'll be here for you. I love you.

My heart started to beat faster. He loves me. I was frozen, staring at these words. So I guess it was time to reveal who I really was. My body shook as I tried to take some deep breaths to calm my nerves. I closed my eyes and tried to find Colin in my mind.

"Nyomi?" I opened my eyes to see Colin standing up from his chair. He looked concerned and scared, which made me even more nervous. He took a step forward and I backed up.

"Before you come closer I need to explain." I said frantically. "I am not from Earth, I am a species from a very similar planet. We came here in search of a new life; but if my species falls for a Human we become bonded. If the bond breaks, I could lose my life." I stood for a moment, terrified to see what he would say next. Colin, without missing a beat, walked towards me. He grabbed me by the waist with one hand to pull me closer to him. With the other hand, he brushed my hair back and looked me in the eyes with a slight smile. My heart started to beat faster as he leaned in and closed his eyes. I closed mine as well and felt his lips touch mine. I sunk into his embrace as I felt a warmth take over my body. As he pulled away and I opened my eyes,

he placed his forehead against mine and whispered,
    "Marry me."

Credits

Although this book is a work of fiction, many of the characters' personalities in the book were based on the author's friends and family. The names below show the character names and the actual names of the people they are based on.

Colin	Aaron White
Megan	Megan Hill
John	John Hill
Rhygel	Isaiah Simmons
Mark	Andrew Marken

Made in the USA
Columbia, SC
10 June 2020